The Banes
of Darkwood

by Maureen Ulrich

Baker's Plays
7611 Sunset Blvd.
Los Angeles, CA 90042
bakersplays.com

FEMALE CHARACTERS

MARJORIE – grew up with the Bane family because her own family was killed mysteriously in an explosion in Lester's lab; now a teacher

ALLISON – Marjorie's friend from teachers' college

AUNT DESDEMONA – long black hair with a silver streak; cold-blooded; does not like anything cooked with garlic; vampire

OLGA – housekeeper/cook

SYLVIA – has not spoken in years; dances ballet; daughter of Desdemona and Lester

WOMAN SELLING FLOWERS

MALE CHARACTERS

HEATHCLIFF – son of Desdemona and Lester; affected by full moons; werewolf

TODD – Marjorie's fiance; a struggling actor who plans to rob her family

UNCLE LESTER – mad scientist

BRUNO – Frankenstein-type character; was created in Lester's laboratory; very protective of Marjorie; talks to plants in conservatory

COUSIN FENWICK – split personality; shell-shocked during World War II; thinks he is Adolf Hitler and Winston Churchill; Desdemona's younger brother

IGOR – hunchbacked family retainer; drags his left leg when moving to the right and right leg when moving left

HIGGINS AND FITZIE – Todd's henchmen

FEMALE OR MALE CHARACTERS

TRAIN CONDUCTOR

ORCHID (may be played by 2 or 3 actors)

PAINTING

VILLAGERS

Scene One

(Forest. Night. Fog.)

*(***HEATHCLIFF*** *stands at center, leaning against his gun, with one foot propped up on a stump.* **IGOR** *stands off to the far left, beckoning to* **HEATHCLIFF** *and making "PSSSST!" noises.)*

HEATHCLIFF. Welcome to Darkwood Estate. *(gestures broadly)* This forest and moor have been in my family for generations. Let me tell you about my family. The Bane family. We… *(looking over at* **IGOR** *in irritation)* What is it, Igor? Can't you see I'm busy introducing the play?

IGOR. You must come home, right away, Master Heathcliff. Lady Bane sent me to find you.

HEATHCLIFF. *(sighing impatiently)* What does Mother want now?

IGOR. I was supposed to let her tell you – but if you must know – Miss Marjorie is coming home tomorrow.

HEATHCLIFF. *(recoiling in horror)* Tomorrow! She's coming home tomorrow? But she can't! She mustn't! *(pulls at his collar and begins pacing)*

IGOR. And why not, Master Heathcliff? Won't you be glad to see Miss Marjorie after all this time?

HEATHCLIFF. *(stopping abruptly at far right)* Igor, do you know what else happens tomorrow?

IGOR. *(scratching his head)* I don't know, Master Heathcliff. Now let me think. *(pauses to reflect)* Is it your birthday?

HEATHCLIFF. *(impatiently)* No! *(puts down his gun, pulls open his shirt and begins scratching at his chest)*

IGOR. Is it Miss Marjorie's birthday?

HEATHCLIFF. No, Igor! *(scratches behind his ear like a spaniel)*

IGOR. *(brightening)* Well then, it must be MY birthday. *(He sings a birthday song.)*

HEATHCLIFF. No! It is not anyone's birthday tomorrow, Igor! It's a full moon!

IGOR. A full moon? *(realizing)* Ooohhhh.

HEATHCLIFF. And you do know what happens on a full moon, don't you?

IGOR. You get hairy, Master Heathcliff. Very hairy. And you grow big teeth – like this. *(puts up two fingers to his mouth to demonstrate)* And your nails grow long and sharp like talons.

HEATHCLIFF. Good for you, Igor. I don't want Miss Marjorie to see me in my – as a – never mind! Run along back to the mansion and tell my mother I'll be late for supper. I need time to think.

IGOR. Lady Bane won't like it, Master Heathcliff. But I'll tell her.

(IGOR exits left.)

(HEATHCLIFF walks to center, deep in thought. As he is bending down to pick up his gun, he suddenly notices the audience.)

HEATHCLIFF. Oh, sorry. I had forgotten about you. *(pauses)* You need to know some of our family traditions. First of all, turn off your cell phones. Secondly, no flash photography. *(picks up his gun and then snaps his fingers as if suddenly remembering something)* Thirdly, please show consideration for other audience members by making as little noise as possible. *(pauses)* Except for laughing. Laughing is definitely allowed. *(laughs demonically)*

(HEATHCLIFF continues to laugh until his voice is drowned out by a train whistle.)

(Blackout.)

Scene Two

(Train station. Morning. Fog.)

(Set: wall with a clock; platform pieces)

(Train whistle.)

*(**MARJORIE**, holding a carpetbag, is standing at center-with **ALLISON**.)*

MARJORIE. Todd promised he would be here in time to see me off, Allison. My train leaves in five minutes.

ALLISON. I'm sure he'll be here, Marjorie. He does clearly adore you.

MARJORIE. *(looking at the clock)* He says he does. But we haven't known each other very long.

ALLISON. Three weeks, isn't it?

MARJORIE. To the day. We met just after *The Times* printed that huge article about my family purchasing the Renoir. *(sets down her carpetbag)* It's hard to imagine Todd can be so certain of his feelings. I'm not.

ALLISON. *(not hearing **MARJORIE**'s last remark)* Imagine! Spending over one hundred thousand pounds on one painting! Your family must be fabulously wealthy!

MARJORIE. *(modestly)* The Bane family are only my adopted family, remember? They took me in after my parents were killed. I was just a child when it happened.

ALLISON. Exactly what did happen, Marjorie – if you don't mind my asking?

MARJORIE. I don't know. Uncle Lester and Aunt Desdemona have always been very secretive about the whole thing. It must have been a horrible accident.

ALLISON. In any case, it's lucky for you that such a wealthy family was willing to raise you. *(pauses)* I have another question, Marjorie, if the Banes have so much money, then what are you doing in teachers' college? You could be living a life of leisure!

MARJORIE. I love children, Allison. And besides that, I want to do something vitally important with my life. *(passionately)* I want to make a difference!

ALLISON. *(cynically)* Well, if I had a choice, I wouldn't be graduating from teachers' college. I'd be marrying someone rich and handsome – like Todd.

MARJORIE. Todd isn't rich, Allison. He's an actor. And actors are always underpaid.

ALLISON. Being handsome is some consolation, just the same. Now, how long will you be visiting your family?

MARJORIE. Just a few days. Aunt Desdemona's letter spoke of a family crisis, but she wasn't specific. I hope Uncle Lester didn't have another explosion in his laboratory.

ALLISON. Laboratory? Your uncle sounds like a mad scientist or something. *(laughing)* Maybe one of your cousins was walled up in the family crypt – or fell from the bell tower.

MARJORIE. *(startled)* I wouldn't make jokes about my family.

ALLISON. And why not?

MARJORIE. *(ominously)* In my family, bad things have a way of happening.

(Train whistle.)

(CONDUCTOR *enters right.)*

CONDUCTOR. Final boarding call for Oxford, Manchester, and York! All aboard that's coming aboard!

MARJORIE. I guess that's that. *(hugs **ALLISON**)* I'll see you when I get back, Allie.

(TODD *enters left, looking worried.)*

ALLISON. Oh, look, there's Todd now!

(MARJORIE *pulls away from **ALLISON** and looks left.)*

MARJORIE. Todd!

TODD. Marjorie!

(MARJORIE *runs towards **TODD** in slow motion and they grasp both hands.)*

(Tumultuous music.)

*(**MARJORIE** and **TODD** gaze into one another's eyes.)*

ALLISON. It's so romantic!

CONDUCTOR. It's bloomin' nauseating, if you ask me. All these lovers' partings in front on me platform! Holds up me schedule! All aboard!

ALLISON. Can't you give them a few minutes? They're in love!

*(**CONDUCTOR** and **ALLISON** both stare at **MARJORIE** and **TODD**.)*

MARJORIE. Oh, Todd, it's wonderful of you to come see me off!

TODD. Just say the word, Marjorie, and I'll come with you. I can't bear to be separated from you. A few days will seem like an eternity.

MARJORIE. *(looking around uncertainly)* It's too soon for you to meet my family. They're not like most families.

TODD. Any family of yours could only be as wonderful as you!

*(**CONDUCTOR** makes a vomiting gesture.)*

MARJORIE. You wouldn't say that if you met my Cousin Fenwick.

CONDUCTOR. For the last time – all aboard!

MARJORIE. Farewell, Todd! *(begins to walk right, waving)*

TODD. Until we meet again, my darling! I hope it will be soon! *(runs towards right, waving)*

*(**MARJORIE** withdraws sadly, exiting right.)*

*(**CONDUCTOR** exits right.)*

*(**WOMAN SELLING FLOWERS** enters left.)*

*(**ALLISON** buys a flower from the **WOMAN** and is engaged in conversation with her for a few minutes.)*

TODD. Now there's a girl who's fallen 'ead over 'eels. *(adjusts his sleeve and removes a small hand mirror from his breast pocket)* And it isn't hard to figure out why. *(looks off offstage and beckons)* Higgins! Fitzie! Come 'ere – I mean – come hither! And make haste, will you?

*(**HIGGINS** and **FITZIE** enter left, running and bumping into one another.)*

Have you got the tickets?

HIGGINS. *(patting his coat pocket)* Yes, gov'na, got em right here.

TODD. And the map?

FITZIE. *(cheerfully)* I got the map! *(feels his pocket and then looks inside nervously)* Well, I did have the map a while ago. Good thing I studied it carefully. I gots it all right up 'ere in me 'ead. *(points at his head significantly)*

*(**ALLISON** finishes her conversation with the **FLOWER WOMAN** and turns to looks at **TODD**. She makes some adjustments to her hair and make-up.)*

HIGGINS. *(smacking **FITZIE** in the back of the head)* I told you to give me the map! But would you listen – no!!

TODD. It doesn't matter, you fools. We can ask for directions to the estate once we get off the train at York.

FITZIE. And how will we know what to steal, Master Warrick?

*(**ALLISON** looks startled and turns away in dismay.)*

TODD. Miss Norbridge can lead us to the valuables. Since she will be so delighted to see me, I shouldn't have any trouble convincing her to tell me all about her family's treasure.

HIGGINS. And will there be lots of treasure to go round, gov'na?

FITZIE. I likes treasure too, Master Warrick!

TODD. *(smiling generously)* We'll split it evenly three ways. Fifty percent for me and twenty-five percent for each of you.

(**ALLISON** *tries to listen without appearing to eavesdrop.*
TODD *catches her looking at him.*)

FITZIE. Twenty-five percent! That's a lot!

HIGGINS. *(smacking* **FITZIE** *in the forehead)* He's cheating us again, you lummox! Just like he did the last time! *(to* **TODD***)* We insist on an equal split, gov'na.

TODD. It *is* even. I get fifty percent, and so do the two of you. What could be fairer than that?

(**HIGGINS** *and* **FITZIE** *stare at one another and scratch their heads suspiciously.*)

You know the plan. Try not to bungle things this time. I've no desire to have Scotland Yard knocking on me door – I mean, *my* door – again. Now, wait over there until the train comes in. *(points to left)*

(**FITZIE** *and* **HIGGINS** *move to left and mime a disgruntled conversation, casting disparaging looks in* **TODD***'s direction.* **TODD** *walks over to* **ALLISON**.*)*

(**ALLISON** *gazes at* **TODD** *nervously.*)

Can I 'elp you, sweetheart? I mean – may I be of assistance?

ALLISON. Why, no. No, you can't. Excuse me. *(begins to walk left)*

(**TODD** *grasps her arm as she walks past and turns her to face him.*)

TODD. Were you listening to us, just now, sweetheart? Didn't anyone ever teach you to mind your own business?

ALLISON. *(stammering)* I – I wasn't listening.

TODD. Let me be the judge of that.

ALLISON. If you don't let go of me, I'll scream!

TODD. As you can see, this platform is deserted, Miss. No one will 'ear you. I mean – it will avail you nothing to scream and make a fuss.

ALLISON. *(bravely)* Does Marjorie know just what kind of a cad you are!

TODD. No, and she's not going to find out. *(beckoning)* Higgins! Fitzie! Come 'ere. I've got another job for you!

(**ALLISON** *screams.*)

(*Blackout.*)

Scene Three

(Bane Manor. Evening.)

*(Set: wood panels; one **PAINTING**; small table at far right)*

*(**IGOR** is dusting the wood panels and notices that the **PAINTING** is looking at him. He tries to catch the **PAINTING** at it a second time but is unsuccessful.)*

*(**OLGA** enters right, carrying a vase full of red roses. She places the vase on the table and begins to arrange the roses. She stands back and looks at the roses critically.)*

OLGA. Something is missing. But vat? *(looks over her shoulder at **IGOR**)* Aren't you finished dusting, Igor? Miss Marjorie will be here any minute.

IGOR. I'm nearly finished, Olga.

*(**OLGA** walks to center.)*

OLGA. Vell, hurry up, vill you? You still need to sweep the scullery and polish the oak table in the dining room.

IGOR. Yes, Olga.

OLGA. And don't forget about mucking out the stables after supper.

IGOR. Yes, Olga.

OLGA. *(walking over to **IGOR** and smacking him in the back of the head)* I've had enough of your cheekiness, Igor.

*(**DESDEMONA** enters left. **OLGA** and **IGOR** immediately stand at attention.)*

DESDEMONA. *(admiring the roses)* Blood red, my favourite. *(smells the roses then looks at them in disgust)* Olga, these roses are far too fresh. You know I prefer them to be musty. Go see Bruno in the conservatory and tell him these ones are entirely unsatisfactory. There must be dead ones somewhere.

OLGA. *(looking offended)* Right away, Madame.

DESDEMONA. And have supper ready for eight o'clock. Remember to set a place of honour for Miss Marjorie.

OLGA. Yes, Madame.

DESDEMONA. And Olga *(pauses significantly)* – no garlic this time. You know that I am *(searches for the right word)* – allergic to garlic.

OLGA. As you wish, Madame.

*(**OLGA** takes vase and exits right.)*

DESDEMONA. Igor, when Master Heathcliff returns from hunting, be sure to polish his boots. He will want to wear them to dinner.

IGOR. Yes, Madame.

DESDEMONA. And Igor – were you the one who forgot to close the blinds in the breakfast room this morning? You know how I feel about direct sunlight!

IGOR. It won't happen again, Madame.

DESDEMONA. Be sure it doesn't.

(Doorbell chimes.)

There's Miss Marjorie now. Quit standing there like a buffoon and go answer the door!

IGOR. Right away, Madame.

*(**IGOR** exits left.)*

DESDEMONA. Just exactly where is one supposed to get good help these days?

*(**FENWICK** enters right, dressed as Adolf Hitler.)*

FENWICK. *(saluting)* Zieg Heil!

DESDEMONA. Fenwick! You're not changed for dinner!

FENWICK. I have thousands of troops along the Eastern front, ready to march on Stalingrad – and you're vorried about dinner?

DESDEMONA. Fenwick, World War II ended five years ago. Adolf Hitler died in a bomb shelter in Berlin. Will you stop this silliness?

FENWICK. *(gesturing wildly)* Nein! Da Führer lives! I AM the Führer! I am Germany!

DESDEMONA. And last week you were Franklin D. Rooseveldt? Fenwick, get changed.

FENWICK. Vun does not tell the Führer how to dress! Vun salutes to show respect for the Führer!

DESDEMONA. Fenwick, go upstairs and get out of those ridiculous play clothes. What will Marjorie think!

FENWICK. *(stamping his foot)* Da Furher does not vant to change! Da Führer vants to vear his uniform!

DESDEMONA. Fenwick, if you do not go to your room immediately, I will take all your toy soldiers down to the scullery and throw them in the woodstove! How will you mount a successful campaign without your troops?

FENWICK. *(shoulders drooping)* Ya vold.

DESDEMONA. And Fenwick – don't forget to wear something – appropriate. *(pinches his cheek)* There's a good little brother.

*(**FENWICK** begins to goose-step right half-heartedly and exits.)*

DESDEMONA. *(calling)* Sylvia! Sylvia! Come down! Your cousin Marjorie is here!

*(**IGOR** enters left, carrying a rolled up newspaper.)*

DESDEMONA. Igor, where is Miss Marjorie?

IGOR. She is not here yet, Madame. My apologies.

DESDEMONA. Then who rang the front doorbell?

IGOR. It was the paperboy, Madame. *(holds out newspaper to **DESDEMONA**, wiping his mouth and rubbing his hands)* He was delicious.

DESDEMONA. *(smacking **IGOR** on the head with the newspaper)* Igor, how many times have I told you – you can't eat the paperboy.

IGOR. Yes, Madame.

DESDEMONA. *(opening the newspaper)* Oh goodness, some poor soul has thrown herself beneath a train at the London station again. Tsk. Tsk.

IGOR. *(peering over **DESDEMONA**'s shoulder)* Was it – a very bloody accident?

DESDEMONA. *(snatching the newspaper away from his view)* There are no pictures, if that's what you mean. *(irritated)* Where is Sylvia? *(calling)* Sylvia! Come down at once! *(to* **IGOR***)* Have you seen Lord Bane?

IGOR. He's in his laboratory, Madame. He did not wish to be disturbed.

DESDEMONA. Yes, yes. I know all that. Some very important experiment, to be sure. *(handing* **IGOR** *the newspaper)* Take this down to him immediately. You know how he enjoys hearing bad news.

IGOR. Yes, Madame.

*(***IGOR** *exits right.)*

DESDEMONA. Sylvia! If you don't come down this instant, I will be very angry with you!

(Doorbell chimes.)

Blast! I'll have to answer it myself!

*(***DESDEMONA** *exits left.)*

*(***SYLVIA** *enters right, tentatively, wearing a white dress. She does a few ballet steps and then darts behind the center panel as soon as* **DESDEMONA** *and* **MARJORIE** *enter.)*

DESDEMONA'S VOICE. I hope you didn't have too much trouble getting a ride to the estate, Marjorie.

*(***DESDEMONA** *and* **MARJORIE** *enter left.)*

MARJORIE. Actually, I had a frightful time, Aunt Desdemona. As soon as I mentioned where I wanted to go, people looked at me as if I had gone mad.

DESDEMONA. The villagers have hated and feared us for generations – or at least ever since your uncle's great great grandfather – *(pauses)* But you know that story as well as I do. Marjorie, we have all missed you so much – especially Heathcliff.

MARJORIE. And I have missed you too, Aunt Desdemona. Some of my happiest memories are here at Darkwood.

DESDEMONA. I'm so sorry no one could meet you at the station, dearest. It's ridiculous that the authorities will not issue a driver's licence to a single member of this family. As if any one of us would purposely veer off the road in order to injure a helpless pedestrian. The thought is preposterous.

MARJORIE. Don't fret, Aunt Desdemona. The milkman didn't mind bringing me here – once I told him that I would walk all the way from the gates. Still, when we pulled in front of the estate, he scarcely gave me time to get my bags out of the trunk.

DESDEMONA. Poor Marjorie, you must be exhausted from your long train ride. Perhaps I could mix up one of my sleeping tonics and you could go lie down.

MARJORIE. *(emphatically)* No thanks! At least, not until you tell me just what family crisis has occurred. I am dying of curiosity.

DESDEMONA. *(looking at MARJORIE)* Dying? What a pleasant surprise! *(pauses)* Oh, you are merely using a figure of speech. *(waving a finger)* You mustn't toy with your auntie's feelings, dearest.

MARJORIE. *(impatiently)* The crisis?

DESDEMONA. *(evasively)* Yes, yes, the crisis. Of course. The crisis.

MARJORIE. There is no crisis, is there, Aunt Desdemona?

DESDEMONA. You have such a suspicious mind, Marjorie. Naturally, there is a crisis. There is always a crisis in this household. You know that.

(SYLVIA peers out from behind the paneling and DESDE-MONA notices her.)

MARJORIE. Aunt Desdemona, I demand to know what –

DESDEMONA. *(interrupting)* Oh look, Marjorie. Your cousin Sylvia has come down to greet you. Sylvia, you remember Marjorie, don't you?

MARJORIE. Hello, Sylvia. You're much taller than I remember. When I left home, you were – what – ten?

DESDEMONA. And now she is thirteen. Isn't she pale and lovely? As pale as death, I always say.

(**SYLVIA** *shyly approaches* **MARJORIE** *and touches her hair and clothing. She takes* **MARJORIE**'s *hat and puts it on her own head, then dances about saucily.*)

MARJORIE. Can she – I mean – has she –

DESDEMONA. Not a word, Marjorie. Not a word at all since that awful day.

MARJORIE. The day of the explosion?

(**SYLVIA** *looks fearfully at* **MARJORIE** *as soon as she mentions the explosion and begins to scream silently. She throws down the hat at* **MARJORIE**'s *feet and jumps on it angrily, then exits, still screaming.*)

DESDEMONA. Oh dear. I must apologize for Sylvia's rudeness. Usually she is much better behaved. (*picks up hat*) I am afraid your hat is ruined.

MARJORIE. It doesn't matter. I shouldn't have reminded her about the – about that day. Maybe I should go talk to Sylvia and –

DESDEMONA. (*taking* **MARJORIE**'s *hand*) Don't worry about her. She'll be all right. Marjorie, it is so wonderful to have you home with us once again. Don't you feel it in your bones – in the pulsing of the blood in your veins? Doesn't it say to you – this is where I belong?

MARJORIE. (*pulling her hand from* **DESDEMONA**'s *grasp*) No, Aunt Desdemona. That is not what it says. It says: "Your aunt is up to her old tricks again. Your aunt wants to shut you up inside the dark walls of this estate, so that you will suffocate and die!"

DESDEMONA. (*delighted*) Oh, Marjorie! How did you guess?!

MARJORIE. (*visibly upset*) This is my life, Aunt Desdemona, and I'll live it the way I want!

(**IGOR** *enters right, still carrying his feather duster.*)

IGOR. Excuse me, Madame.

MARJORIE. Igor! How wonderful to see you again! You – haven't changed a bit.

IGOR. Thank you, Miss Marjorie. *(to* **DESDEMONA***)* Lord Bane was wondering if you might come down to the laboratory for a few minutes.

DESDEMONA. Can't it wait?

IGOR. Lord Bane was most insistent, Madame.

DESDEMONA. *(impatiently)* Very well. Please excuse me, Marjorie. I will be right back. Perhaps you would like to go out to the conservatory. Bruno has been experimenting with some interesting species of carnivorous flora.

MARJORIE. I would love to see Bruno again. But when you return, Aunt Desdemona, you WILL tell me about the crisis – whatever it is.

*(***MARJORIE*** exits right.)*

*(***IGOR*** stares at ***DESDEMONA*** expectantly.)*

DESDEMONA. *(noticing* **IGOR***'s critical expression)* What? What did I do?

IGOR. It's not for me to say, Madame.

DESDEMONA. You are so right about that, Igor.

IGOR. Even so, Madame, isn't it time Miss Marjorie was told – the truth?

DESDEMONA. I will tell her when the time is...suitable. *(pauses)* In the meantime, Igor, be sure to send Master Heathcliff to the conservatory as soon as he returns from hunting. He will want to get reacquainted with Miss Marjorie.

IGOR. Yes, Madame.

DESDEMONA. And don't forget to take Miss Majorie's bags up to her bedroom. And do something about this, will you? *(hands* **IGOR** *the hat)*

IGOR. Yes, Madame.

*(***DESDEMONA*** exits.)*

IGOR. *(putting the hat on his head and attempting to imitate* **DESDEMONA***)* Do this, Igor. Do that. Miss Marjorie is coming. Miss Marjorie is special. Miss Marjorie is a royal pain in the –

*(***HEATHCLIFF*** enters.)*

HEATHCLIFF. What's that you said about Miss Marjorie, Igor?

IGOR. *(starting guiltily and putting the hat behind his back)* Nothing, Master Heathcliff.

HEATHCLIFF. *(pointing)* What is that you're hiding, Igor? *(snapping his fingers)* Give it to me this instant.

*(**IGOR** holds out the hat and then takes it back. **HEATHCLIFF** jumps and pants excitedly like a dog, trying to get the hat, then visibly struggles to regain control of his doglike impulses. He holds out his hand commandingly and **IGOR** reluctantly gives him the hat.)*

(reverently) She's here, isn't she, Igor? Somewhere in this house. *(looks about excitedly)* I must find her! *(sniffing the air)* I can smell her perfume! Does she still look as beautiful, Igor?

IGOR. *(shrugging)* If you like beautiful girls, Master.

(Doorbell rings.)

*(**IGOR** sighs and exits left.)*

HEATHCLIFF. *(walks to left and begins pacing impatiently)* Marjorie – here – at last! Do I dare speak to her – when already I can feel the confounded curse taking hold? *(scratches his neck in a dog-like manner)* How could she love me – when I am such a – a monster?

*(**HEATHCLIFF** throws back his head and howls, then abruptly puts his hand over his mouth.)*

IGOR'S VOICE. But sir, you can't come in. Madame told me not to let anyone in without –

TODD'S VOICE. I am a close friend of Miss Marjorie Norbridge. My name is Todd Warrick. Is Marjorie here?

*(**TODD** and **IGOR** enter left.)*

HEATHCLIFF. *(demanding)* Who are you?

TODD. *(putting his hands on his hips)* And who are you?

HEATHCLIFF. I asked first!

TODD. My name is Todd Warrick. I'm an actor – on London's West End.

HEATHCLIFF. *(folding his arms across his chest)* I've never heard of you.

TODD. I'm a friend of Marjorie's. *(pulling himself up bravely)* In fact, Marjorie is my betrothed.

HEATHCLIFF. *(cocking an eyebrow)* Oh, she is, is she?

TODD. You still haven't told me who you are. *(striking a thoughtful pose)* If I were to hazard a guess, I'd say that you are her cousin Heathcliff. *(adding sarcastically)* Her childhood playmate.

HEATHCLIFF. I'm not actually her cousin. Marjorie is – not a blood relation. Her parents –

TODD. *(waving a hand and walking to far right)* Yes, yes. I know the story. They were killed in an accident.

HEATHCLIFF. *(ominously)* Is that what she told you? *(walks to center)*

TODD. *(defensively)* Yes. Isn't that the truth?

HEATHCLIFF. *(laughing)* The truth? You want the truth? My friend, you can't handle the truth!

TODD. I demand to see Marjorie at once.

HEATHCLIFF. Marjorie is unavailable – just at the moment.

TODD. *(spying the hat in **HEATHCLIFF**'s hand and grabbing it from him)* She was wearing this hat when I saw her off at the train station. Has some ill befallen her, you scoundrel? If you have 'urt her – hurt her – in any way, you shall know my wrath! *(tosses hat to left)*

*(**HEATHCLIFF** chases after the hat and picks it up in his teeth, then brings it back to **TODD** and looks at him expectantly.)*

TODD. If you do not take me to her, I shall be forced to call the local authorities. *(looking around)* You do have a telephone here, don't you?

HEATHCLIFF. *(blankly)* A telephone?

TODD. Indoor plumbing?

*(**HEATHCLIFF** shakes his head.)*

Electricity?

*(**HEATHCLIFF** shakes his head.)*

TODD. *(cont.)* Well, what amenities do you have?

HEATHCLIFF. *(cunningly)* Too numerous to mention. A famous actor such as yourself will be treated with great hospitality during your stay at Darkwood. Igor, please show this gentleman to our… *(pauses dramatically)* finest guestroom. Master Warrick, I'll let Marjorie know that you are here.

TODD. *(smiling in satisfaction)* That's better!

IGOR. Please – walk this way.

*(**IGOR** exits left, limping and shuffling. **TODD** shrugs and imitates **IGOR**'s limp and shuffle.)*

TODD. *(pausing before the **PAINTING** at center)* I say, old chap. Just who is the person in this portrait?

HEATHCLIFF. It is my great great great grandfather.

TODD. Just what's a painting like this worth?

HEATHCLIFF. *(laughing)* No one would buy that painting, Master Warrick!

TODD. I can't shake the feeling it's been staring at me.

HEATHCLIFF. Oh really? I can't imagine what gave you that idea.

*(**TODD** exits left.)*

*(**HEATHCLIFF** laughs.)*

*(**PAINTING** laughs.)*

(Blackout.)

Scene Three

(Conservatory. There is a long table at center with a few strange looking potted plants. A few tall plants stand in the background. One is a huge **ORCHID** *at far right beneath a tarp. There is a window at left.* **BRUNO**, *wearing a white apron, is repotting a plant.)*

BRUNO. *(speaking to the plant)* There, there, my pretty. You be much happier in your new home. *(holding up plant to admire it)* Must make lots of pretty blossoms for Miss Marjorie. *(pauses and holds plant up to his ear)* Yes, my pretty. Miss Marjorie coming home today. *(holds plant up to his ear again)* No, mustn't tell Miss Marjorie the secret. Miss Marjorie must never know. *(pulling plant up by its roots)* Bad pretty.

(**MARJORIE** *enters left while* **BRUNO** *is speaking and listens curiously.)*

MARJORIE. Hello, Bruno. And just what is Miss Majorie not supposed to know?

BRUNO. *(jumps in surprise, holds up the plant, and waves a finger at it anxiously)* Mustn't tell, pretty! Mustn't tell! *(turns his back towards* **MARJORIE***)*

MARJORIE. *(walking to* **BRUNO** *and standing beside him)* Tell me, Bruno. I'm your friend, remember? You and Heathcliff and I were childhood playmates.

BRUNO. *(stuffing the plant in the pocket of his apron and muttering distractedly)* Mustn't tell! Mustn't tell!

MARJORIE. *(touching* **BRUNO** *gently on the arm)* I'm sorry, Bruno. I didn't mean to upset you. You can tell me later – when it's safe – all right?

BRUNO. *(sighing in relief)* All right, Miss Marjorie.

MARJORIE. Now, give me a hug to welcome me home.

(**BRUNO** *turns to face her with arms outstretched but doesn't touch her with them when* **MARJORIE** *hugs him warmly.)*

MARJORIE. I have missed you, Bruno. *(drawing away and surveying the table)* What have you been up to while I've been away at school? Growing more flowers?

BRUNO. *(spreading his arms proudly)* Pretty ones, Miss Marjorie.

MARJORIE. Very pretty ones indeed, Bruno. *(gesturing at tarp)* What's that over there?

BRUNO. No! *(grabs **MARJORIE** by the arm and pulls her back)*

MARJORIE. Oh, I won't hurt it, Bruno. I just wanted to get a closer look.

BRUNO. Miss Marjorie NEVER go near that pretty flower. NOT EVER.

MARJORIE. It must be of the carnivorous variety. Aunt Desdemona did mention something about that. *(playfully smacks **BRUNO** on the upper arm)* You've been a very busy boy while I've been gone, Bruno.

*(**BRUNO** gives **MARJORIE** a playful smack which knocks her down.)*

BRUNO. Sorry, Miss Marjorie. *(helps her back up)*

MARJORIE. That's all right, Bruno. I had forgotten just how strong you are. Now tell me all about these plants. *(points at the plants on the table)*

*(**BRUNO** proudly pantomimes describing each plant while **MARJORIE** looks on interestedly.)*

*(**HIGGINS** and **FITZIE** appear at the window and peer in, pointing at **MARJORIE** and staring at **BRUNO** in horror. **BRUNO** and **MARJORIE** do not notice them.)*

*(**HEATHCLIFF** enters left.)*

*(**HIGGINS** and **FITZIE** duck and disappear from view.)*

HEATHCLIFF. Hello, Marjorie.

MARJORIE. *(noticing **HEATHCLIFF** and reacting with shock)* Heathcliff!

HEATHCLIFF. *(smiling)* Welcome home.

MARJORIE. Heathcliff, you gave me such a start. This is so totally unexpected, I – I hardly know what to say!

(fanning herself)

HEATHCLIFF. And why not? Am I so rrrrrrr- repulsive?

MARJORIE. No – on the contrary – you have become quite handsome.

HEATHCLIFF. *(turning away momentarily)* Yes!!

MARJORIE. Bruno, would you mind leaving Heathcliff and me alone for a few moments? We have some catching up to do.

*(***BRUNO*** exits left, grumbling.)*

MARJORIE. *(moving towards* **HEATHCLIFF***)* I'm so glad to see you. I've missed you – and Aunt Desdemona and Uncle Lester.

HEATHCLIFF. Of course.

MARJORIE. There is a question I must ask you, Heathcliff.

HEATHCLIFF. Yes?

MARJORIE. Why didn't you respond to any of my cards or letters?

HEATHCLIFF. *(sighing)* I could not.

MARJORIE. And why not? Are you involved? Is there someone else?

HEATHCLIFF. There is no one else, Marjorie. You know that. I wish I could say the same for you.

MARJORIE. *(putting her hands on her hips)* What do you mean?

HEATHCLIFF. *(scratching his chest impatiently)* Please forget I said that. Marjorie, I need to talk to you about something.

*(***BRUNO*** enters left, carrying another potted plant.)*

BRUNO. *(holding up the plant proudly)* Another pretty.

HEATHCLIFF. Do you mind, Bruno? Miss Marjorie and I are having a serious conversation.

*(***BRUNO*** waves a hand and goes behind his table.)*

HEATHCLIFF. *(pulling at his collar)* Marjorie, what do you know about the family...curse?

MARJORIE. Curse?

HEATHCLIFF. *(walking to the window and looking out)* The moon is nearly up. I have to goooooo. *(howling loudly and shaking his head)*

MARJORIE. Heathcliff, what on earth are you doing?

HEATHCLIFF. We'll talk again – soooooon.

    *(**HEATHCLIFF** exits left, howling.)*

MARJORIE. Heathcliff, where are you going? *(to **BRUNO**)* He really is the most exasperating man!

    *(**MARJORIE** exits left, running.)*

    *(**BRUNO** shrugs and holds up his plant for inspection.)*

BRUNO. There, my pretty. *(The plant slips out of his hands and smashes on the floor)* Ooopsie!

    *(**BRUNO** exits left.)*

HIGGIN'S VOICE. Coast is clear, Fitzie! Let's go!

FITZIE 'S VOICE. Right you are, Higgins!

    *(**FITZIE** and **HIGGINS** enter right.)*

HIGGINS. We've got to find Master Warrick! 'e must be here somewhere!

FITZIE. *(triumphantly)* I wants to show him me map!

HIGGINS. Fat lot of good it'll do us in this huge mansion, Fitzie. Now start lookin' for 'im. *(walks behind table and looks underneath)*

FITZIE. Shouldn't we be lookin' for treasure too, Higgins? You knows how I likes treasure!

HIGGINS. *(still looking)* So you keep tellin' me, Fitzie. You haven't given me a moment's peace since we climbed over the garden wall.

FITZIE. A piece of cake that were, right Higgins? Just like Master Warrick said it would be.

HIGGINS. *(sighing)* And speakin' of Master Warrick – get lookin'!

FITZIE. Right! *(pulling tarp off of **ORCHID**)* Nothing 'ere but a great big shrubbery, Higgins.

HIGGINS. *(not looking)* Keep lookin'!

FITZIE. *(worriedly)* Should we tell Master Warrick about the rumours? *(walks to left and makes a feeble effort at searching his surroundings)*

HIGGINS. *(walking to right and answering distractedly)* What rumours, Fitzie?

FITZIE. Oh, you didn't 'ear 'em I guess. But I did. Yes, good old Fitzie didn't miss a thing.

HIGGINS. *(turning and facing **FITZIE**)* What are you talking about?

FITZIE. *(puffed up with his own importance)* This be a wicked, wicked place, Higgins. The villagers say Lord Bane does frightful experiments in his labratory.

HIGGINS. *(exasperatedly)* Fitzie, what else did you hear?

FITZIE. *(looking around)* Well, there's the bit about the… *(pauses dramatically)* big doggie?

HIGGINS. *(blankly)* Big doggie?

FITZIE. They says Lord Bane's son goes out 'unting every-day with his wolfhound.

HIGGINS. *(sighing in relief)* Oh.

FITZIE. Then at night, the young gentlemen turns into a werewolf. He howls at the moon, he does.

(Wolf howl.)

*(**HIGGINS** shudders and staggers right, bringing him close to the **ORCHID**.)*

FITZIE. Sort of like that.

HIGGINS. *(unimpressed)* That's poppycock! There ain't no such thing as a werewolf!

FITZIE. Well, that's good news – 'cause that means there can't be no vampire in the Bane family neither!

*(**ORCHID** grabs **HIGGINS** and puts a leaf over his mouth. **HIGGINS** struggles violently.)*

(not noticing the struggle) There's also a full moon this evenin. Maybe robbin' this here family ain't such a good idea, Higgins. *(pauses and turns)* Higgins? *(noticing at last)* Higgins!

HIGGINS. *(freeing his mouth for a moment)* Would you mind 'elpin' me, you great oaf?

(**FITZIE** *rushes to right and engages in a tug-of-war with* **ORCHID** *over* **HIGGINS**. **HIGGINS** *and* **FITZIE** *both scream repeatedly for help.*)

(**BRUNO** *enters left, carrying a broom.* **BRUNO** *pauses for a moment to size up the situation, then hits* **ORCHID** *with the broom until it releases* **HIGGINS**. **FITZIE** *helps* **HIGGINS** *to his feet, but they do not notice* **BRUNO**. **BRUNO** *covers* **ORCHID** *with tarp.* **HIGGINS** *and* **FITZIE** *move towards center.*)

FITZIE. Are you all right, Higgins?

HIGGINS. *(patting himself and examining his hands)* Yes, Fitzie, old pal. I'm fine. Thanks to you and – this gentlemen. Thanks, Mister. *(turns to right and extends his hand in* **BRUNO**'s *direction)*

(**BRUNO** *turns around.*)

(**HIGGINS** *screams and faints.*)

FITZIE. What's wrong, Higgins? You look like you saw a – *(sees* **BRUNO** *for the first time)* MONSTER!!! *(faints)*

(Blackout.)

Scene Five

*(Laboratory: There is a raised chair located at center, which is covered with a white sheet. **TODD** is seated in the chair. **UNCLE LESTER** is standing beside the chair, holding a set of booster cables. A cart with an electronic device and a newspaper stands next to him.)*

*(**LESTER** wears a white labcoat and rubber gloves and is holding up a syringe.)*

*(**DESDEMONA** stands on the other side of the chair.)*

DESDEMONA. I don't want to watch another one of your experiments, Lester dear. And besides – *(looking at her wrist-watch)* It's going to make dinner very late.

LESTER. Don't you want to see if my new truth serum works, Mona darling? It would mean so much to me.

DESDEMONA. *(reluctantly)* Very well.

LESTER. Wonderful! I'll awaken my subject first.

*(**LESTER** pulls away the sheet with a flourish, revealing **TODD**.)*

*(**TODD** is unconscious, his head tilted over to the side. **TODD** wears a metal cap on his head and a long coiled wire is attached to the electronic device. His wrists are strapped to the chair.)*

DESDEMONA. *(impatiently)* Will it take long?

LESTER. No. He just needs a little…jump start.

*(**LESTER** attaches the booster cables to the metal cap and turns the knob on the device.)*

(Loud crackling sound.)

(Smoke.)

*(**TODD** jumps about in the chair and awakens.)*

LESTER. There. That's better.

DESDEMONA. Hurry up and give him the injection, will you?

LESTER. *(plunging the needle into **TODD**'s exposed arm)* There!

TODD. Ouch! *(moaning)* Oh, me 'ead. The last thing I remember was that hunchback taking me to my room and giving me something to drink. And now – I'm here. Where am I?

DESDEMONA. Tell him, Lester.

LESTER. *(gesturing grandly)* Welcome to my laboratory! I am Lord Bane, Master of Darkwood. You may call me – *(pauses dramatically)* Lord Bane. And you are?

TODD. *(turning to* **DESDEMONA***)* Todd Warrick. And you must be Marjorie's Aunt Desdemona.

DESDEMONA. Charmed, I'm sure. Now, correct me if I'm wrong, but you introduced yourself to my son Heathcliff as Marjorie's betrothed. Is that right?

TODD. Yes. But I was lying. Marjorie and I are not engaged.

LESTER. *(delightedly)* Do you see? It works!

DESDEMONA. Yes, Lester dear. You know – there really isn't room in our family tree for someone of your profession just at this moment. What did you say you did for a living?

TODD. I'm an actor. But I'm not a very good one. *(pauses)* Why did I say that?

DESDEMONA. An actor. Right. *(pulling back* **TODD***'s head to better expose his neck)* I just need to determine your blood type. If you don't mind, I'll take a teeny-weeny sample.

LESTER. *(putting a hand in* **DESDEMONA***'s face and pushing her away gently)* Not so fast, Mona. I have other plans for this subject.

DESDEMONA. *(placing her hands on her hips)* Lester!

TODD. What plans? *(tries to move his arms for the first time)* Why am I strapped to this chair? *(panicking)* What's going on?

LESTER. Just a little experiment. I hope you don't mind.

TODD. You're insane!! What have you done with Marjorie?

DESDEMONA. Now, now, Mister Warrick. All this concern for Marjorie is a bit of an ACT, isn't it?

TODD. Yes, it is. *(shaking his head)* Why do I keep telling the truth?

DESDEMONA. In fact – the only thing you really love is Marjorie's money.

TODD. Yes!! *(shakes his head again)* I mean – n-n-n. Why can't I lie? I'm usually very good at it.

(BRUNO enters right, holding FITZIE and HIGGINS by their collars. They are struggling and whimpering.)

FITZIE. Let me go, you big lummox!

HIGGINS. Don't make him angry, Fitzie! He's a lot bigger than both of us!

DESDEMONA. Bruno! What have you got there?

LESTER. I believe you know these two gentlemen, Mister Warrick?

TODD. I hired them to help me rob your estate.

LESTER. I see.

HIGGINS. Tell 'em we didn't mean any 'arm, govna'!

FITZIE. *(sniveling)* It was your idea to rob this 'orrible place, Master Warrick! I never wanted any treasure, I did!!

DESDEMONA. Maybe they need a shot of your truth serum, Lester dear.

LESTER. That won't be necessary. What should we do with these two thieves, Mona?

BRUNO. Pretty is hungry.

DESDEMONA. We can't have that, can we? Feed them to your pet, Bruno.

HIGGINS & FITZIE. *(staring at one another)* No!!

(BRUNO exits right with HIGGINS and FITZIE, still struggling helplessly.)

TODD. *(to DESDEMONA)* I can explain everything – if you'll just let me! *(noticing her fangs)* Have you ever considered having a dentist file down those teeth?

DESDEMONA. *(putting her hands on her hips)* The truth can become quite annoying after a while.

TODD. *(to LESTER)* Please don't kill me!

DESDEMONA. Shut him up for a moment, will you Lester? He's getting on my nerves.

LESTER. Mine too.

    (**LESTER** *turns the dial on the electronics device.*)

    (*Crackling sound.*)

    (*Smoke.*)

    (**TODD** *passes out.* **LESTER** *covers* **TODD** *with the sheet.*)

DESDEMONA. That's better.

    (**SYLVIA** *enters left, leaping.*)

Sylvia! What are you doing down here? You know that you're not allowed in your father's laboratory!

    (**SYLVIA** *begins miming angry people, shaking their fists and climbing the garden walls.*)

What's that you're saying, dear?

    (**SYLVIA** *continues miming a battle scene and collapses dramatically on the ground at the end.*)

That's a very nice dance, dear. Very original, I must say. And quite unusual.

    (**SYLVIA** *stands up and extends her hands pleadingly towards her parents.*)

LESTER. Is there something else, Sylvia? You do look upset.

    (**SYLVIA** *backs away to the left, beckoning to them desperately.*)

    (**SYLVIA** *exits left.*)

DESDEMONA. That was most peculiar, wasn't it?

    (*Angry shouting.*)

LESTER. Do you hear that?

DESDEMONA. Yes. Do you suppose it's the neighbours again?

LESTER. That would be most inconvenient.

    (**IGOR** *enters left, breathlessly.*)

DESDEMONA. Igor, can you tell us what's going on out there?

IGOR. *(gasping for breath)* It's the villagers, Madame! They've climbed the walls!

DESDEMONA. Oh bother! Don't they know it's dinnertime! Igor, go tell them to come back tomorrow. Or better yet – tell them not to come back at all. I am tired of their petty grievances.

IGOR. Tell them yourself, Madame! I'm getting out of here!

(IGOR exits left, limping and shuffling.)

DESDEMONA. *(putting her hands on her hips)* That's gratitude for you!

(FENWICK enters left, gesturing wildly. He is dressed as Sir Winston Churchill.)

FENWICK. We will never surrender! We will fight them in the air! We will fight them on the beaches!

LESTER. That's the spirit!

DESDEMONA. Fenwick, tell those pests to go away.

FENWICK. *(abruptly dropping his role)* Who?

DESDEMONA. The villagers, Fenwick! They're storming the mansion again!

FENWICK. Really? *(shouting)* Retreat! Retreat! Run for your lives! It's every man for himself!

(FENWICK exits left, still shouting.)

LESTER. *(scathingly)* Coward! How could he possibly be your brother, Mona darling.

DESDEMONA. That's so sweet of you, Lester.

VILLAGER #1's VOICE. *(offstage)* Let's look for them down here!

VILLAGER #2's VOICE. *(offstage)* Wait till I get a piece of them!

VILLAGER #3's VOICE. *(offstage)* Death to the Banes!

LESTER. Now what?

(VILLAGER #1 enters left. He is followed by HEATH-CLIFF, who wears a werewolf mask. His arms are tied

behind his back and **VILLAGER #2** *holds tightly to his arm.* **MARJORIE** *wears a gag and* **VILLAGER #3** *has her arms pinned.)*

DESDEMONA. Take your hands off my son! Release him this very instant!

*(***HEATHCLIFF*** snarls and snaps at ***VILLAGER #2***.)*

VILLAGER #2. Hey, he bit me, he did! He's 'ad his shots, ain't he?

LESTER. He most certainly has not!! What are all of you doing in my laboratory! Get out of here! This is a place of science!

VILLAGER #1. We've 'ad enough of your experiments, Lord Bane!

VILLAGER #2. Yeah! We wants satisfaction this time!

VILLAGER #3. We're sick of the strange goings-on in this 'ere 'ousehold!

DESDEMONA. I don't know what you're talking about!

VILLAGER #1. Oh, you don't do you? Well, we caught this woman digging in our village cemetery!

VILLAGER #2. And your son was in me flower beds again! He's dug up me prize begonias for the third time!

VILLAGER #3. And he's bin 'owling outside my window all night long! How's a body supposed to get any sleep with all that racket!

VILLAGER #1. And don't forget about me rubbish bins! He's knocked 'em over again! Who's going to clean up that mess, I want to know?

VILLAGER #2. This is the last straw, I tell you! 'Ow would you like it if some beast did this in your backyard every night?!

DESDEMONA. Did you say that Marjorie was in the cemetery? Do you know what this means, Lester?

LESTER. Yes, Mona darling.

*(***DESDEMONA*** retreats to far right, deep in thought.)*

VILLAGER #2. *(demanding)* What are you going to do about me begonias?

LESTER. I'll give you some cuttings – from Bruno's prize roses. Will that appease you?

VILLAGER #2. *(scratching his head)* It might.

LESTER. I could also offer you the most sincere apology for my son's behaviour.

DESDEMONA. Lester! You can't apologize! We're aristocrats! Aristocrats don't apologize to riff raff!

VILLAGER #1. Just 'oo are you callin' riff raff, Lady Bane?

LESTER. *(to Villagers)* I promise you'll never be bothered by my family again.

VILLAGER #2. *(suspiciously)* Not ever?

LESTER. You have my word on it.

VILLAGER #1. That's better. Untie them, Clovis.

(**VILLAGER #2** *unties* **HEATHCLIFF**. **VILLAGER #3** *removes* **MARJORIE***'s gag.*)

MARJORIE. *(running to* **DESDEMONA***)* Aunt Desdemona, it was horrible! I don't know what's come over me!

DESDEMONA. *(enfolding* **MARJORIE** *in her arms)* It's all right, my dearest Marjorie. Your uncle and I will explain everything.

LESTER. Heathcliff will show you to the conservatory. I think you'll find some of the botanical specimens there quite – *(pauses dramatically)* gripping.

VILLAGER #3. Don't you be lettin' him out again. We won't be so easy on 'im next time.

LESTER. I'll try to remember.

(**HEATHCLIFF** *and* **VILLAGER #1, 2,** *and* **3** *exit right.*)

DESDEMONA. *(still holding* **MARJORIE***)* Good riddance to them.

LESTER. Marjorie, are you hurt?

MARJORIE. No, just terribly confused, Uncle Lester. Why do I suddenly feel the desire to – to – *(breaking down and sobbing)*

DESDEMONA. Don't upset yourself, Marjorie. It's time we told you the truth.

MARJORIE. *(looking up and wiping her eyes)* The truth?

LESTER. *(pulling a handkerchief out of his labcoat pocket and handing it to* **MARJORIE***)* Your aunt and I can't keep it from you any longer, Marjorie.

*(***MARJORIE*** blows her nose loudly in the handkerchief.)*

MARJORIE. *(handing* **LESTER** *the handkerchief)* Well – for goodness sakes, tell me! I've waited long enough!

DESDEMONA. Your parents didn't die in an explosion.

MARJORIE. Then what DID happen to them?

*(***LESTER*** and **DESDEMONA** *look at one another.)*

MARJORIE. Tell me!

LESTER. Nothing happened to them, Marjorie.

MARJORIE. Nothing? What do you mean nothing? If nothing happened to them, then WHERE ARE THEY?

*(***LESTER*** and **DESDEMONA** *look at one another again.)*

DESDEMONA. You don't have any parents, Marjorie. Not in the normal sense of the word.

MARJORIE. *(backing away towards center)* That's not possible!

LESTER. It is for me – *(gesturing grandly)* – and my laboratory.

MARJORIE. *(shaking her head)* What are you saying?

DESDEMONA. Your Uncle Lester made you, Marjorie, right here in this very room – nearly nineteen years ago.

MARJORIE. I don't believe you! The only THING you ever made in this laboratory was – Bruno!

DESDEMONA. Bruno was merely the first, dearest.

LESTER. *(holding up his arms)* You were my greatest creation!

DESDEMONA. Do you see what this means, Marjorie? You belong here – with your family! You truly are one of us!

MARJORIE. *(backing into* **TODD***'s chair)* No!

*(***TODD*** moans loudly and moves under the sheet. **MAR-JORIE** starts and jumps away from the chair.)*

MARJORIE. *(distracted)* What's under that sheet? Another one of your creations?

(**DESDEMONA** *and* **LESTER** *exchange glances.*)

DESDEMONA. Marjorie, calm yourself. Your uncle and I need to explain something else to you.

MARJORIE. *(hysterically)* I've had enough of your explanations! I want to see for myself!

LESTER. *(warning)* You'll be sorry.

(**MARJORIE** *pulls back sheet and gasps.*)

MARJORIE. Todd?

(**TODD** *groans and lets his head fall back.*)

MARJORIE. What are you doing here?

TODD. *(dreamily)* Marjorie?

MARJORIE. Did you follow me here – after I told you not to?

TODD. *(dreamily)* Yes, my darling.

MARJORIE. Are you all right? *(pulls sheet away so that she can see him more fully)* Did anyone hurt you?

LESTER. As you can see – he's quite unharmed. All in one – er – piece.

MARJORIE. Uncle Lester, I demand you release him at once.

DESDEMONA. I'm afraid your uncle can't agree to that. Tell Marjorie what you've been up to, Todd.

TODD. *(suddenly realizes he isn't dreaming)* You!!

DESDEMONA. Yes, it's me. Tell her, Mister Warrick.

TODD. *(sobbing)* I can't!

(**DESDEMONA** *and* **LESTER** *both fold their arms and wait.* **TODD** *hangs his head for a moment, then gestures to* **MARJORIE** *with his finger. She takes a step closer. He gestures again. She sighs loudly and stands beside him, bending her head down to his mouth.* **TODD** *whispers in her ear.*)

MARJORIE. *(straightening up)* You what?!

TODD. I wasn't going to take very much – just everything I could lay my hands on.

MARJORIE. *(disbelieving)* Todd, how could you rob my family?!

TODD. It was easy. I don't love you at all. And as for your family – they're all freaks!

MARJORIE. They are not!

DESDEMONA. Lester, are you going to stand by while he insults the Bane name?

LESTER. Certainly not! *(takes a step towards the cart)* A lethal dose of electricity should shut him up for good.

MARJORIE. *(holding up her hand)* Wait!

TODD. *(imploringly)* Marjorie? Will you save me?

MARJORIE. Be quiet, Todd. I need time to think.

> *(**MARJORIE** leans against cart, deep in thought.)*

> *(**OLGA** enters left.)*

DESDEMONA. What is it, Olga? Can't you see we're in the middle of a family crisis?

> *(**MARJORIE** notices the newspaper under the cart and picks it up, scanning the front page at first casually then with increasing perturbation.)*

OLGA. *(visibly annoyed)* Madame, dinner is cold.

DESDEMONA. Of course it is, Olga. It's nearly midnight.

OLGA. Do I have Madame's permission to put it away and clear the table? *(yawning)*

DESDEMONA. Of course, Olga. Then go to bed.

> *(**OLGA** exits left.)*

> *(**MARJORIE** screams.)*

LESTER. What is it, Marjorie?

MARJORIE. *(dropping the newspaper)* It's Allison! She's dead!

DESDEMONA. *(blankly)* Who is Allison?

MARJORIE. My dearest friend! I said farewell to her just this morning…at the train station. *(suddenly realizing)* Todd…you were there too.

TODD. I killed her.

MARJORIE. *(gasping)* Murderer!

TODD. I didn't do it myself! Fitzie and Higgins did most of the dirty work.

MARJORIE. Fitzie and who?

DESDEMONA. Never mind, Marjorie. They've been taken care of.

LESTER. We can do the same for Mister Warrick. Just give the word.

MARJORIE. No. *(carefully explaining)* Killing is wrong, Aunt Desdemona.

DESDEMONA. Who told you that nonsense?

TODD. *(emphatically)* It's definitely wrong to kill people. Unless they get in your way of course.

LESTER. *(shrugging)* What are we going to do with him if we don't kill him? We can't have him going down to the village and stirring up the populace again. We've had quite enough trouble with them already.

*(**HEATHCLIFF** enters left.)*

TODD. Here's another freak.

*(**MARJORIE** smacks **TODD** in the head with the newspaper.)*

DESDEMONA. Heathcliff, darling. You've been a naughty boy again, haven't you?

HEATHCLIFF. Mother… Father… I need to speak with Marjorie – alone.

LESTER. Hmm. Sounds serious.

HEATHCLIFF. It is serious, Father.

MARJORIE. Heathcliff, anything you have to say, you can say in the presence of your parents.

HEATHCLIFF. All right. *(takes a deep breath)*

MARJORIE. I'm waiting, Heathcliff.

HEATHCLIFF. Marjorie, I'm a werewolf. *(closes his eyes and clenches his fists, as if expecting a blow)*

*(Everyone stares at **HEATHCLIFF**.)*

TODD. Well – duh.

MARJORIE. I know you're a werewolf, Heathcliff. And I don't care.

HEATHCLIFF. You don't?

MARJORIE. Of course not. Would it bother you to know that I'm – that I was –

HEATHCLIFF. Assembled in this very laboratory using the parts of dead people? What possible difference could that make to me?

MARJORIE. Oh, Heathcliff!

HEATHCLIFF. Marjorie!

(*Tumultuous music.*)

(**MARJORIE** *runs to* **HEATHCLIFF** *and they embrace.* **HEATHCLIFF** *throws back his head and howls.*)

HEATHCLIFF. I suddenly feel like going out on the town! Care to join me?

MARJORIE. I'd love to!

(**HEATHCLIFF** *and* **MARJORIE** *begin to exit left.*)

DESDEMONA. Wait a moment!

(**MARJORIE** *and* **HEATHCLIFF** *turn to face her.*)

Don't do anything your father and I wouldn't do.

HEATHCLIFF. Right, Mother.

(**MARJORIE** *and* **HEATHCLIFF** *exit left.*)

LESTER. Mona, I'm starving. Let's go make a sandwich.

DESDEMONA. What a wonderful idea!

(**LESTER** *and* **DESDEMONA** *begin to walk left.*)

TODD. Are the two of you just going to leave me here?

LESTER. (*stopping in his tracks*) I'd forgotten about him.

DESDEMONA. (*sighing*) So had I.

(**LESTER** *and* **DESDEMONA** *move so that they are standing on either side of* **TODD**'s *chair.*)

TODD. I'll do whatever you say – for a while at least! Then I'll just try to kill you both and rob your estate after all!

DESDEMONA. You know – he's not much danger to us as long as he keeps on telling the truth.

LESTER. You're right about that, Mona darling.

DESDEMONA. Maybe you could use him around the laboratory. You're always complaining that you don't get enough help.

TODD. *(brightly)* I can be very helpful...when I'm not being lazy.

LESTER. *(snapping his fingers)* I know! I could attach an arm – right in the middle of his chest. I really could use an extra hand around here. *(to* **TODD***)* Will that be all right with you?

*(***TODD** *stares at him, speechless.)*

LESTER. Great! We'll get started in the morning.

DESDEMONA. You're a genius, Lester darling.

LESTER. Let's go get that sandwich now, Mona. I'm famished. Turn off the light for me, will you?

DESDEMONA. I'd be delighted. *(waves at* **TODD***)* Nighty night!

*(***DESDEMONA** *flips a switch on the panel. Stage darkens. She and* **LESTER** *exit left, as spot remains on* **TODD***'s shocked face, then grows gradually smaller.)*

(Blackout.)

COSTUMES

MARJORIE: suit jacket and skirt or flowered dress, pumps, hat, purse, gloves.

AUNT DESDEMONA: black dress (long, form-fitting). Cape, long black wig with silver streak, very pale, red lips.

TODD WARRICK: suit, tie, white shirt, fedora.

ALLISON: flowered dress, hat, purse, gloves, pumps.

UNCLE LESTER: lab coat, messy white wig (Albert Einsteinish), dark pants, tie, white shirt, handkerchief and syringe in pocket, very pale.

BRUNO: grey or green suit jacket, black turtleneck/crew neck, Frankenstein mask, dark pants and shoes, white apron.

HEATHCLIFF: white shirt, dark pants and boots, werewolf mask.

FENWICK: light brown shirt, black tie, swastika armband, black pants and shoes (Adolf Hitler); suit jacket, white shirt, tie (Winston Churchill).

IGOR: black tail coat, white shirt, pillow tucked under shoulder to create hunchback; ugly tie, black pants and shoes.

HIGGINS: turtle neck, suit jacket, dark pants and shoes, toque.

FITZIE: sweater, dark pants, hat with ear flaps.

SYLVIA: white calf-length dress; white nylons, white ballet slippers, white ribbon in her hair, very pale, red lips.

OLGA: black blouse and ankle length skirt, apron, feather duster.

FLOWER WOMAN: shawl, dark skirt, hat, gray wig.

CONDUCTOR: black baseball cap, dark suit jacket and pants, white shirt, dress shoes.

VILLAGER #1: house coat and night cap, pajama bottoms.

VILLAGER #2: house coat, slippers, hair down.

VILLAGER #3: house coat, slippers, big bosom, hair in curlers tied with a scarf.

PLANT: green turtle neck, green streamers, headdress made of vines.

PAINTING: suit jacket, tie, dark pants, white shirt.

SET

Scene Two
Clock
Platform

Scene Three
Wood panels
Frame for Painting
Small table

Scene Four
Stone panel with window
Long table

Scene Five
Stone panel
Chair with metal cap, booster cables, long coiled cord
Cart with electronics equipment
Smoke machine

PROPS

Scene One
Gun
stump
lantern

Scene Two
Carpetbag
Flower
Hand mirror

Scene Three
Feather duster
Vase of roses
Rolled up newspaper
Hat

Scene Four
Potted plants
Tarp
broom

Scene Five
White sheet
Newspaper
Syringe
Rubber gloves
Rope
Gag
Werewolf mask

OTHER TITLES AVAILABLE FROM BAKER'S PLAYS

SAM SPUD, PRIVATE EYE

Maureen Ulrich

9m, 6f / Comedy, Jr. High/High School / Simple set

Sam Spud, Private Eye is a parody of the cheap detective novel. Sam Spud is a down-on-his-luck private eye with a fondness for junkfood and cliches. He is convinced that his down-to-earth secretary Jane Reynolds has a crush on him. Lula Baum-Schell, a gorgeous former model and actress, hires Sam to help find her husband, Edward, a wealthy dogfood magnate. Police detective Inspector Oiseau complicates matters because he hates Sam for making him smell bad in the "Velveeta Cheese" case. Will Sam be able to solve this case before the kidnappers kill Edward? Your guess is as good as ours! A fun, silly noir-style comedy that high schools could really have a blast with!

www.ingramcontent.com/pod-product-compliance
Lightning Source LLC
Chambersburg PA
CBHW070421120726
47909CB00005B/1747